For Dan, who builds beautiful roads
—S. L. H.

For my dad
—E. S.

 LITTLE SIMON

An imprint of Simon & Schuster Children's Publishing Division
1230 Avenue of the Americas, New York, New York 10020
Text copyright © 2017 by Susanna Leonard Hill
Illustrations copyright © 2017 by Erica Sirotich
All rights reserved, including the right of reproduction in whole or in part in any form.
LITTLE SIMON is a registered trademark of Simon & Schuster, Inc., and associated colophon
is a trademark of Simon & Schuster, Inc.
For information about special discounts for bulk purchases, please contact Simon & Schuster
Special Sales at 1-866-506-1949 or business@simonandschuster.com.
The Simon & Schuster Speakers Bureau can bring authors to your live event. For more information
or to book an event contact the Simon & Schuster Speakers Bureau at 1-866-248-3049 or visit our
website at www.simonspeakers.com.
Designed by Chani Yammer
Manufactured in China 0517 RKT
10 9 8 7 6 5 4 3 2 1
This book has been cataloged with the Library of Congress.
ISBN 978-1-4814-9546-2
ISBN 978-1-4814-9547-9 (eBook)

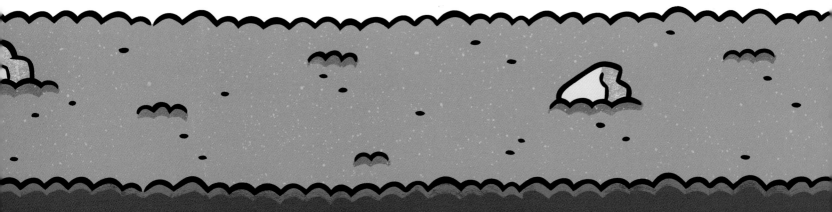

THE ROAD THAT TRUCKS BUILT

by Susanna Leonard Hill   illustrated by Erica Sirotich

LITTLE SIMON

NEW YORK   LONDON   TORONTO   SYDNEY   NEW DELHI

This is the traffic
that's moving too slow.
Cars and buses have nowhere to go.

What is the answer?
I'm guessing you know.

The trucks
need to build
a new road!

Building a road's more than one truck can do.

It's such a big job,
it requires a crew!

This is the **BULLDOZER**,
first on the site,

to shove rocks away
with all of its might
to make way for the road
that trucks built.

This is the SCRAPER
whose sharp metal blade

forges a new path through
forest and glade

to make way for the road
that trucks built.

This is the **GRADER**
whose leveling blade

smooths out the roadbed
and evens the grade

to make way for the road
that trucks built.

This is the **PAVER**
who spreads out the track
of steaming hot asphalt,
all bubbly and black,

to make way for the road
that trucks built.

This is the ROLLER
with steel drums so great
they flatten the asphalt
till it's smooth as slate

to make way for the road
that trucks built.

This is the **PAINT MARKER**
spraying with care
the yellow and white lines
from here to there

to make
way for the road
that trucks built.

Look! Now it's completed!
A road smooth and new,

with wide open lanes,
cars and buses drive
through.

After the PAINT MARKER sprayed with care
the yellow and white lines from here to there . . .

After the ROLLER whose steel drums so great
had flattened the asphalt as smooth as slate . . .

After the PAVER had spread out the track
of steaming hot asphalt, all bubbly and black ...

After the GRADER's broad leveling blade
had smoothed out the roadbed and
evened the grade . . .

After the SCRAPER whose sharp metal blade had forged a new path through both forest and glade . . .

After the BULLDOZER, first on the site,
shoved rocks away with all of its might . . .

to make way for the ro

A guide to the trucks:

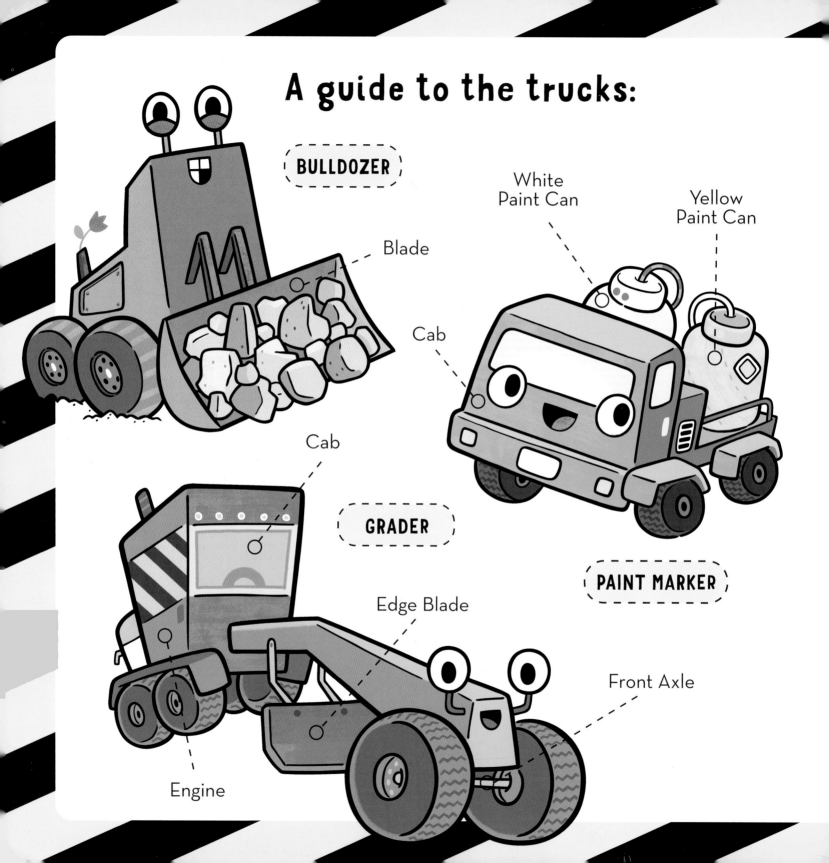

BULLDOZER

Blade

White Paint Can

Yellow Paint Can

Cab

Cab

GRADER

Edge Blade

PAINT MARKER

Front Axle

Engine

SCRAPER

Hitch

Cab

Bowl

ROLLER

Cab

Front Roller

Front Axle

Tractor Unit

Cab

Hopper

Screed

PAVER